# Double Bubbles

Based on the series created by John Tartaglia
Based on the TV series teleplay written by Rachel Lipman
Adaptation by Liza Charlesworth

Houghton Mifflin Harcourt
Boston New York

## Download FREE music from Splash and Bubbles!

Download two tracks from
*Splash and Bubbles: Rhythm of the Reef*
*(Songs from Season One)*
by visiting **www.splashandbubblesmusic.com**
and entering the code: SPLASHMUSIC

Available for a limited time only.




ISBN: 978-1-328-98665-8 paper over board
ISBN: 978-1-328-97344-3 paperback

hmhco.com

Printed in China
SCP 10 9 8 7 6 5 4 3 2 1
4500728527


Jim Henson
The Jim Henson Company

It was a perfect day to play hide-and-seek! Ripple searched the reef for her friends. At last, she spotted one.

"Gotcha, Bubbles!" she shouted.

When the fish swam out of her hiding spot, Ripple was surprised. Bubbles was not her usual pink color. She was green!

"Who's Bubbles?" asked Bubbles.

Ripple thought Bubbles's voice sounded different too. So not only had Bubbles turned green and changed her voice, but she didn't even know her own name!

Ripple darted off to find Splash and Dunk.

"It's Bubbles," she said. "She's different. She's acting all weird, and . . . and green!"

"How do you *act* green?" asked Dunk.

Now everyone was confused.

Suddenly, Bubbles popped out from a hiding spot.

"Here I am!" she said.

She was pink. It was Bubbles, all right!

"This doesn't make sense," said Ripple. "If Bubbles is here, then who was the other fish?"

Swish! A green fish swam up.

"Do you mean *me?*" she asked. "I'm Finny."

Wow! Bubbles and Finny sure looked alike.

"See, guys?" shouted Ripple. "I was right. There *are* two Bubbleses!"

**FIN FACT:**
Mandarin dragonets live in reefs and can be many different colors and patterns.

"Excuse me, but there's only *one* of me," said Bubbles.

"And only *one* of me," said Finny.

**FIN FACT:**
Mandarin dragonets don't have scales. Instead, they produce an icky slime that coats their bodies and protects them from disease and predators.

"You guys *do* have a lot in common," said Splash.

They both had long tails and fancy fins. They both made slime to protect their skin.

"That's because we're both Mandarin dragonets!" said Finny.

"Wow, we are a lot alike," said Bubbles.
"You want to play with us?"
"I'd love to!" said Finny.

Finny played finball with the gang.
She was a natural.
*Almost* as good as Bubbles.

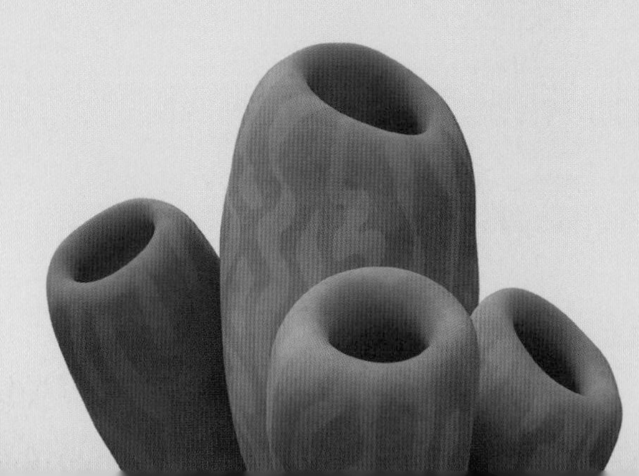

Next, they visited the mud pit.

"This mud puddle looks fantastic!" Finny said.

"Finny loves glop and gloop as much as you do, Bubbles!" Splash said. "It must be so great having a friend just like you."

Bubbles should have been thrilled. She'd found a fish who liked finball and mud as much as she did. And her friends really liked Finny too.

But for some reason, Bubbles felt sad.

After a while, Ripple swam by and noticed that Bubbles looked unhappy.

"Something wrong?" asked Ripple.

"It's kind of . . . Finny," answered Bubbles.

"You don't like Finny?" Ripple asked.

"I do! But she's *just like me*," said Bubbles. "Now that there's a brand-new Bubbles, why does anyone need me anymore?"

"But there can't be a new Bubbles!" said Ripple.

Ripple told Bubbles that even though her 499 brothers *looked* alike, each brother was special. Number 342 told great stories. Number 96 made the silliest faces. Number 77 always slept next to Ripple.

"So, even though Finny and I look alike on the outside, it doesn't mean we're the same on the inside," Bubbles said with a smile.

"Of course not!" said Ripple. "You're *our* Bubbles."

"I bet Finny could use a friend," said Bubbles, "being the new Mandarin dragonet in Reeftown."

Bubbles felt better. When they played capture-the-shell, Bubbles and Finny were teammates. They found more shells than Splash and Dunk!

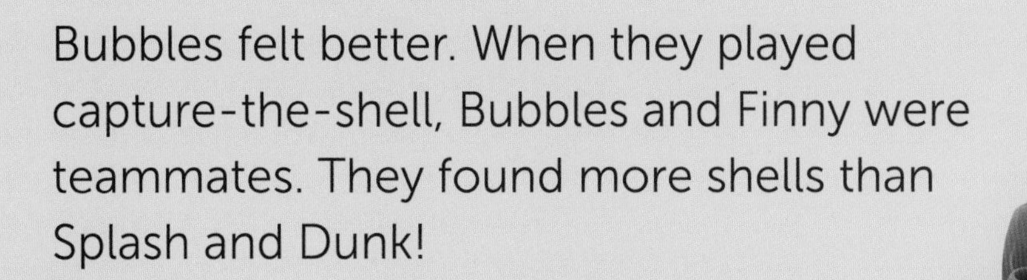

**FIN FACT:**
Mandarin dragonets flap their fins very quickly, so they hover in place like ocean hummingbirds!

Bubbles had made a fabulous new friend. It was too bad Finny was only visiting Reeftown. She and her family were leaving soon for their home reef.

"I hope you'll come visit," said Finny.

"Definitely!" said Bubbles. "C'mon—how about one last dip in the mud pit?"

"Thought you'd never ask!" said Finny. "Let's go."

Yucky, ucky, slimy, grimy!

They dove and splashed and rolled around until they were both covered in mud.

Maybe they splashed
a little *too* much!

Bubbles and Finny got so muddy that their friends couldn't tell them apart.

"That's okay—*we* can," said Bubbles.

They were alike, but different too. And that's the perfect way for friends to be!